Breath of Dragons

For Aoife

best wishes

Andy Allan   *Andy*

Aug. 2015

Indigo Dreams Publishing

First Edition: Breath of Dragons
First published in Great Britain in 2015 by:
Indigo Dreams Publishing Ltd
24 Forest Houses
Halwill
Beaworthy
EX21 5UU
www.indigodreams.co.uk

ISBN 978-1-909357-77-8

British Library Cataloguing in Publication Data. A CIP record for this book can be obtained from the British Library.

Designed and typeset in Palatino Linotype by Indigo Dreams.

Cover design by Ronnie Goodyer at Indigo Dreams.
Printed and bound in Great Britain by 4edge Ltd.
www.4edge.co.uk

Papers used by Indigo Dreams are recyclable products made from wood grown in sustainable forests following the guidance of the Forest Stewardship Council.

for landscape and love

Acknowledgements

A huge thank you to:

Morag, Eileen Carney Hulme, Helen Addy and Carol Argyris, all my forWords friends for their endless encouragement, advice and unstinting support

Dawn and Ronnie at Indigo Dreams, for their belief and for the opportunity

All my friends for their generosity, constructive criticism and camaraderie

Also, thanks to John Glenday and the many other poets and friends I have met in recent years for their kindness and their sage advice.

I am exceptionally grateful to the editors of Causeway/Cabhsair, Reach Poetry, The Dawntreader, Sarasvati, Poetry Scotland, Poetry Cornwall, The Larcenist, NorthWords Now, the StAnza Poetry Map of Scotland, The Wait (cancer support anthology) and the Moniack Mhor anthology.

CONTENTS

An Iolair Mhòr (The Great Eagle)

'Coh-bac, coh-bac, coh-bac, coh-bac.'
Startled grouse voice their alarm
on the high path up over Lag Buidhe.
Swooping down the hillside,
they brush the ragged slopes
awash with racing cloud-shadows.
Wind-built waves of heather sweep
across a tweed-green sea.

North beyond the Spey,
over forested hills and moors,
the distant lowlands of the Laich
lie under a blurred blue haze.
A dark speck spirals high in icy skies
as I rest my weary legs to watch and reminisce.
'Iolair Mhòr your days of greatness have gone,
Your clan is small, the world has turned.'

Oidhreagain clings tightly to the ground,
its presence reminding me that even now
there are still things I can only name in Gaelic.
Rising, breathing deeply, I crest the shoulder,
raise my eyes to the great dark silhouette.
'Oh Iolair Mhòr, our day is done,
torn away with the tattered leaves of history.
Chaos laps at our feet, washing ever-higher,
drowning the memories.'

I shiver under passing clouds as
the distant eagle wheels to leave and
two heather-skimmers glide down into oblivion
repeating their timeless call;
'Coh-bac, coh-bac, coh-bac, coh-bac.'

Oidhreagain is Scots Gaelic for cloudberries.

The Highland Cottage

Defiant speck of white in this immensity,
proudly enduring, against all odds.
Surrounded by wild beauty and desolation,
resisting the weighty heavens
and the ignorant dark.

The brooding past is always close,
a lingering legacy in the ceaseless rain.
Two tattered, air-whipped rowans,
remain on duty before a flaking door
considering their memories, and pain.

The land is infused with prompts and clues
unseen by most who reach this place,
the white rose sheltering by the crumbling wall
perhaps the most tangible hint
for those who read the sign.

The white rose was the badge of the jacobites.

This Land

Strangers, aching for certainty and control,
full of empty confidence,
search for meaning they cannot find
in a land beyond comprehension,
a brooding, barren emptiness that
reflects their expectations,
unforgiving, hostile, cold and grey.

It caresses with a hand they cannot feel,
murmurs melodies they cannot hear,
yet to other eyes this land is ablaze with life
and passion so fierce, it sears the soul,
a land so lovely, it rends the hearts
of its children and dwells in them forever.

Its promises whisper through empty glens,
wander between the weeping peaks,
connections beyond understanding.
Our souls will always wander here
brushing the memories of generations,
our hearts responding to her ceaseless call.
This is our land. We are the land.

Going Back

Wet shards of shiny slate
lie scattered on the doorstep
strewn like confetti death-petals.
A battered birch crouches
by the crumbling cottage,
hiding from the rampant wind.
The dark lochan broods,
squally showers pass over,
light-sparkles dancing
on its rippling furrows.
Hesitation, a moment's pause,
brows narrow at the lingering
presence of the gnarled rowan.

The dim interior calls to me,
tempting with memories.
Split and squint,
a broken silvered door
hangs from one rusty hinge.
Thin strips of faded blue
cling in the deepest grain,
holding on to yesterday.
Bracken's spring growth
moistly curls in welcome,
each pale finger memory-pointing
to my rose-tinted past.

*Superstitious Highlanders often planted a rowan at their doorway where its
protective properties could ward off witches.*

Why America?

Summer sparkled in Glenfiddich.
You were an insolent ten,
with a laugh that skipped
through breeze-rippled alders,
warm winds caressing the air.
Pale hair-strands floated, free,
danced to the river's drone.
It's pibroch smooth in memory,
water-washed as the round,
white boulders you grew among.
The footbridge, wooden, silvered,
clad in blue-green lichen,
cast a dark shadow over the gurgling ford.
You knelt in the sun's sharp dazzle,
plucking the yellow flowers with care.
Your scowl captured in a shutter-click.

Breath of Dragons

The pumping throb of currents
races over rugged seas
of rank, dank heather.
Powerful, probing storms
swirl and rush,
grazing grey crags
where lurking eagles slide.
Moist and tantalizing fragrances
swirl beneath brooding skies,
caressing russet hill-sides.
The breaths of western dragons
swoop and soar;
mountain flanks teased,
lashed with life's moist kisses.

The Hare

Startled grouse swoop,
their alarm, like sonic pebbles,
rattling down sombre,
wind-rippled slopes.
A warming breeze ruffles heather,
black-tipped ears snap skywards,
nostrils flare, re-tasting air.

A brown head lifts,
eyes widening as smoke-tastes
slither and surround.
Blood pounds as sinuous white
curls and concentrates
in ever-thickening shrouds.
Immobilized, confused,

anchor-clamped to soil.
Fire's crisp crackle,
crawls closer,
revokes terror's spell,
fleet feet sailing,
heartbeat racing,
bursting finger-snap free.

Mist in Glen Einich

Glen Einich weeps.
The rushing brown burn
tumbling grey boulders,
thrums her eternal lament,

sliding between hags of hanging
heather and yellowed grasses.
White foam swirls to her timeless song,
her grating voice ceaselessly rumbling.

Stifling grey encroaches,
caressing dark and crumbling crags.
Ice-cold fingers crawl over peaks
and passes, endlessly aching for warmth.

Reaching for the moor's rough floor,
sinuous wisps hang from a seething ceiling.
Furtive shadows gather.
Stones rattle in veiled corries.

Mournful echoes define the colourless day.
Briefly, a pale disc shimmers overhead,
but a stag's muted roar rends the moment.
Light's fleeting promise fades.

Legacy

Her pale hand lifted through shafts
of summer light to graze my cheek.
'You are like your father, you have his eyes.'
A silent, glinting tear gathered
in helpless, sighed acceptance.
Raw words tumbled from her heartache.
'He'd want you to have it.'
The jacket was a perfect fit.
Discomfort increased.
I could hear his whisky-breath,
smell his rasping whisper,
his obstinate truth,
'I am like my father.'
His wraith-eyed smile meandering
through sepia memories
caressed the child I was.

After the Summer Rain

Sooty, black-stained buildings
bathed in smoke's pungent tang,
rouse reminders of childhood
and a grimy world, unsullied.
Rafts of yellow pine-needles
sweep across slick paving
in a riot of ripples.
Freshness drips from
crisp green leaves,
flickering light-patterns
daze and dazzle.
Spouts of water gurgle
from gaps in rotten masonry,
reflections pour from puddles,
drowning the murky present.
Aromas tease through
innocent days of damp delight,
a freedom to take risks,
drizzle dribbling on sweaty skin,
wet hair plastered on contentment.

Wisdom

I was always told to listen carefully
to those who knew better, that
teachers and grown-ups are always right.

He threw the yellowed shaws aside
and plunged the fork into the naked ridge,
lifting, straining through the crumbling earth.
I watched, poised and ready,
with the expectant eyes of a six-year-old,
as my father unearthed treasure
and dropped it at my feet.
I pounced on the new tatties and
carefully dropped each purple prize,
with the clunk of success,
into a white, chipped, enamel bowl
then took them in to Mam.

Next day at school we
heard about stars and planets,
Mrs. Pirie said the Earth
turned over and over so fast
that no-one could see it move.
I often squatted by the garden
after that, watching, waiting.
She was right.
I never saw the earth move yet,
but I often wondered why
weeds didn't fall out
while it was churning over.

The Gathering Storm

A malevolent stain crawls overhead.
The neutered sun succumbs,
slipping through seething shrouds.
Trees shiver in gathering gloom
Tension grows, feeding on unrest.
The anxious forest waits.

Cawing darkness flaps from a dead tree.
A chill breeze builds,
tearing raggedly through branches.
Leaves swirl in death-rattle dances.
As nervous fledglings rush for cover
boughs heave obeisance to chaos.

Pale promise grows aloft,
the balance shifts.
The deflating wind sighs in
growing silvery brightness.
Tension eases, light prevails,
Ragged cloud-scraps flee.

Warm recovery soaks into the land,
a joyous blackbird sings of peace.
Old crow, dark eyes calculating,
resumes her eternal watch,
quietly accepting the ignorance
and gullibility of youth.

Descent

Venerable oak,
mossy knees concealing
roots, deep-delving digits,
winding down through
generations of dust.
Furtive fluttering breaths of breeze,
the languid slip through leaves
of murmured promises;
caressing minds with nagging,
half-glimpsed secrets.
Beneath hoary, ancient arms
a toddler with dirty, digging fingers
squeals with joy, ensnares me.
His beaming dust-streaked face,
expression enigmatic, daring,
laughs and teases me
with my grandfather's eyes.

Beside the Fluttering Well

No respite from searing sun
in sultry, sticky air.
Lapping green shade beckons,
promising cool, dark sanctuary.
A wood-pigeon repeats his mantra
while myriads of tiny insects drone.
Perceptions slip as familiar scents
of summer forest fill the air.

A dry stick snaps somewhere
beyond possibility,
thick air gathering around the pool.
Neck hairs rise as skin tightens.
Dark water waits, expectant, still.

Colour bleeds from rags
on sagging branches as
they flutter their silent secret.
On the tree-top, unmoved,
unchanging, ever watching,
sits Crow,
dark creature of the void,
guardian of this shrine.
As a lone bee hums indifference,
logic fails, and strangely,
I feel closer to the old ways now.

Small packages, gifts for the gods, were often tied to trees beside a holy spring.
This practice still endures in some places.

Blackbird

I become aware of your presence,
a slight shadow of movement
ghosting on perception's edge,
lurking amongst strawberry plants.
Nosy, inquisitive, self-seeking,
we are not so different.
You cluck softly, almost like a hen,
as you hop forward a few feet
wait and cluck again, impatiently
demanding that I step aside.
No sudden movement!
I ease the blade into soft soil,
wait, lean on my spade
sink into wonder,
watch your ritual of approach.
I echo your call and smile
as you cock your head.
Re-assured, you bounce forward
to signal approval of my efforts,
and to inspect my diggings.
I might as well be invisible.
Head turned, expectant,
you listen to the crumbly soil,
forage around my feet,
frantically scratch-kick the ground,
tiny granules tumble
to reveal succulent delights,
and, perhaps more telling,
our ability to ignore all else
in the pursuit of what we want.

Solstice Wood

Ethereal spirits waft
among barren boughs,
weaving through mystery,
slipping between gnarled fingers,
in dim and dwindling light.

Bathed in sun's red descent,
leaves tumble through branches,
jaundiced and black-spotted,
drifting to the vast cathedral floor
where hungry foragers scrape.

Slithering through vaulted silence,
veiled presences lurk,
obscure and unmentionable,
inhuman eyes roving, probing,
intelligent, consuming, dark.

More than breeze as dank air moves,
a pigeon flaps alarm,
its feathered clatter freezing time,
merging shadows splinter
and disappear with ease.

Storm Coming

Vague signals posted on whispers,
in gathering gloom the sea wakes
to the keening of a wheeling gull.
Her skin wind-roughens through moments,
massive swells restraining coiled menace.
The grumble of her growing awareness
beach-rumbling with the incoming tide.
Shingle grates and rattles
as she surges, deep and green.
Indistinct grainy hills lurk
in the low shrouds of distance.
Salt air grows heavy,
invasive scatterings of chameleon grey
smudge blue-sky's early sparkle.
Rumours soar on dream-raked air,
sliding, rapture-teasing vibrations.
Anticipation whistles on the wind,
the freshness of excitement's edge.

The Clearing at Abriachan

Whistle-whipped winds rip
rampant peaks of spruce,
stark pines stand dark
in frigid misty air,
trembling amidst chaos.
Jagged splinters of shattered kin
pierce the pitiless February sky,
an affirmation of Winter's anger.
Wooden shards lie silver-scattered,
forest bones laid bare.

A leafless rowan looms
through soft and fading light,
angular limbs and stretching fingers
silhouetted on pale wooden buildings
squatting in an oasis of calm.
Sunlight teases the creaking timber
dissolving the cabins into belonging.
Hysterical blackbirds punctuate
the muffling silence as a
great spotted woodpecker punches
his claim on the classroom wall.

Imbolc

Dark heaving silhouettes stand stark
in winter's low-slung sun.
Dislodged snow-dust
swirls on drafty gusts.
Angry air pushes, whooshes,
tears at tossing tops.
Below, in pale and fading light,
a dark-green place of windless drips,
dank silence cloaks exposed damp roots,
on soggy, mossy floor.

Tiny tree-buds tremble
through frigid forest drear,
anticipating change.
New beginnings, subtle stirrings,
faint warmth and growth of light.
A snowdrop shoot breaks cover,
a potent promise rising,
birthing teasing whispers
of hope a-new.

Eyes Too Deep

Time drifts through this ancient wood,
with dust motes and idle thought.
At clearing's dappled edge I sit
in golden grasses, listening as
languid trees seduce me.
Sun-wrapped, pristine, pure,
scent as sweet as laughter,
as if this world has just begun.

Warm afternoon spins teasing promise
through taste-tangled air,
but when the silent singing stops
I raise my head, and there sits hare,
wary, wise, watching,
eyes as deep as river drawing mine
to depths so dark, elation falters, dies.
His memories wash through me,
the past dripping through abstraction,
seeding empathic tears
as discord shudders through
trembling trees.

Distant shouting, chainsaw's roar,
birdsong ceases, hopelessness gathers,
a shadow falls in clear bright day.
Hare's eyes find mine, guilt rises,
humanity's shame floods through me,
and when again I lift my head,
all depth of wonder's flown,
I find I sit here empty, all alone.

It was believed that when a god wished to spy on humans he took the form of the hare.

The Pool of All Knowledge

Like the tired shadows of day's end
his need-to-know hangs.

A tumbled grey dyke,
lichen-stained with greeny-blue,
lies desolate among dark ranks of nettles.
The burbling burn slaps mossy stone,
its song, a long soft murmur.
In flickering thick, green light,
the Willow loiters,
hunched on his root-riddled bank.
Above the peat-stained pool
where knowledge lies,
he broods in the patient shade,
his bobbing fingers knocking
on a window of liquid sepia.
Rippling circles widen,
encroach on a glistening rink
where insects flit and skate.
Swallows skim the mirrored surface,
seething clouds of midges bustle
in muggy shadow.
Old Willow waits,
patience on his shoulder,
desire blackens his mind.
Silver flickers dart in still, dim depths.
The pool's heart is shattered
in a flash of feathery blue.

The salmon, knowing all there is,
says nothing.

*In Celtic mythology, the salmon was the keeper of all knowledge; the willow
was identified with the dark spirit of Wisdom.*

Death on the Beach

Wind's teeth tear at the sky,
rip the warmth from the day.
Pounding breakers bludgeon
Culbin's shifting sands,
stalking her exposed northern shore.
Undermined dunes collapse
into churning salt-water chaos,
trees totter on the crumbling edge,
fated to join the salt-whitened bones
of kin as they lie strewn
on the kissed-clean strand.
Some endure, pointing skywards
like warning eldritch fingers.
Grey seals, insulated in strange,
accept that death is inevitable
and sprawl at this wounded edge
unassailable in their icy isolation.

Minus Forty

Sun-kisses sparkle
in harsh bright silence.
Angular birches stand
in naked solitude,
limbs glinting in the light.
Drooping pines,
burdened with white,
squat motionless
beneath an ice-blue dome.
Poised in expectant torment,
they await the splintering cracks.

Minus forty degrees is the temperature at which trees freeze and burst open.

These Enduring Hills

Memories of dryad guardians
still linger in this landscape;
an elder race, imbued with
wisdom of the journey,
the ceaseless cycles of life and death.
Brooding patiently, life-joy dwindling,
huddled down damp and dreary,
they wait for their time to come again.
Years pass into grey yesterdays,
thoughts fixed on ancient forests
in a distant past.

Waiting for a New Day's Dawn

Tendrils of woodbine creep into light,
their rippling search,
sifting the leaves of book,
the pages of story.
No guardians from elder days
remain to guide saplings
through their growth decades,
none have survived
to teach and protect them
as they struggle to awareness.
Witnesses with little hope
ponder the ancient shaman's tales,
memories encoded in soft rings,
in the pathways of fungi-filament
that form the forest's heart and soul:
such delicate, fragile strands,
injured beyond bearing,
mangled, ripped and torn,
by axe and fire and plough.
Deep-rooted survivors stand and watch,
waiting for a change in the wind.

Red Sentinel

Tough proud, enduring witness,
she has watched through passing time,
the lives of generations flow
beneath this hoary pine.

Red sentinel standing tall and stark,
matriarch of her kind,
around her feet, mere ants, we crawl,
the "Faer-world" out of mind.

That mirror world, that echoes ours,
where energies merge and flow,
oblivion is lurking there,
much closer than we know.

Around her crown dark-watchers glean
the news from far and near;
the Morrigu . . . whose dealings are
in darkness, death and fear.

Flapping, ancient rags of black,
and raucous, chilling cries,
denizens from that other place
where illusive myth-worlds lie.

Omnipotence eludes their grasp,
venerable though they be,
oblivious of their sentient host,
primordial, silent, free.

Dark-seekers sliding betwixt worlds,
their transient passing marked,
recorded deep in ancient rings,
'neath ragged, time-worn bark.

A constant presence in our midst,
enduring, dark and deep,
observing and absorbing this
unconscious world, asleep.

The Morrigu was the Celtic goddess of war, fate and death. The carrion crow was her favourite disguise.

The Forest's Prayer

On whispers of wandering winds
waft me the pollen of friends,
and gentle rains of summer.

On woodland fringe,
in deep, green glades,
let grass grow lush and sweet,
and contented grazers grow fat,
that saplings may rise untoothed,
to the bright light and the high skies.

Keep fire at bay, if you can,
and the destroyer, man.

Indigo Dreams Publishing
24 Forest Houses
Halwill
Beaworthy
Devon
EX21 5UU
United Kingdom
www.indigodreams.co.uk